Penelope Murch is a 'weak crew' who can helm a boat at sea, but mostly daydreams away in the cockpit. This trip from the Isle of Bute to the Isle of Skye was her great adventure. It has been woven into a fantasy tale for children, initially to interest her grandchildren who sail with her, two at a time. Penny lives with her husband on a farm in the middle of England and has a conservatory full of beautiful plants and spiders that abseil down onto unwary friends! She is an expert on rhododendrons and cultivates a quintessentially English garden assisted by a busy flock of guinea fowl and Hazel, the golden retriever.

RASCAL

Penelope Murch

AUSTIN MACAULEY PUBLISHERS™

LONDON • CAMBRIDGE • NEW YORK • SHARJAH

Copyright © Penelope Murch (2021)

A CIP catalogue record for this title is available from the British Library.

ISBN 9781528985314 (Paperback)
ISBN 9781528985321 (ePub e-book)

www.austinmacauley.com

First Published (2021)
Austin Macauley Publishers Ltd
25 Canada Square
Canary Wharf
London
E14 5LQ

To my good friend, Carol. We had such fun together writing and illustrating these stories for our grandchildren. "There is a story in that!" she would say and collapse into laughter.

CHAPTER 1

Eva-three-tons-only lives in the Kyle of Bute. She is attached to the seabed by a heavy chain because she is a buoy and her job is to hold onto a sailing boat in the summer.

She holds on tightly in a gale and then, when the sun comes out and the wind slackens, she and her boat swing together as the tide takes them gently up the Kyle, and then back again as it turns.

Eva-three-tons-only loves her boat. His lines are so elegant, his paint shines in the sun, the mast reaches for the sky, and his long heavy keel beneath the waves keep his passengers safe. Eva calls him her little brother.

One night, a sea urchin who lived at the bottom of Eva-three-tons-only's chain left his home and climbed up. He sat on Eva's round orange head and stared around him in amazement.

"Careful," said Eva, "you are sticking your heels in my eyes."

"Sorry," said the urchin and grabbed her hook instead. "Look at the stars in the sky," he said, "and all these beautiful boats bobbing up and down on the water. The rocks at the water's edge, the soft greens of the hills coming down to meet them. And I can see sheep grazing and grass blowing in the wind. What a wonderful world up here."

And with that he swung himself up and over onto Eva's boat. He landed on the bows with his feet apart and stretched his arms high up towards the sky. He turned, jumped down into the cockpit, then ran back up again. Suddenly he stopped and peeped into the little window on the side.

Inside was a little house, a cooker, a sink, cupboards, and shelves full of tins of food. There were two bunks for sleeping with a thin table in between.

"Awesome." He said to himself.

"The Skipper is coming to my boat tomorrow," said Eva, "then he will sail away, my little boat looks forward to that."

"Really?" said the urchin, "Where will he go?"

"I never know until he comes back, but I know he wants to go to the Isle of Skye."

CHAPTER 2

So next day, when he heard the Skipper climb aboard his boat, the urchin swarmed up the chain, climbed on to Eva-three-tons-only's head, and jumped into the cockpit.

"Hello," he said, "I have come to help you sail your boat."

"Well I never!" said the Skipper. "And who are you?"

"I haven't got a name, but I am a sea urchin."

"I see," said Skipper looking amazed, "Well I never did! You can come with me, I will be glad of your help and I'll call you Rascal, because you are so cheeky. Clip yourself on Rascal and we will set sail for the Isle of Arran."

"Is that the way to the mighty ocean with rolling waves?"

"Yes, that's right."

"I don't need to clip on, I live in the sea, and the sea doesn't bother me."

"But the boat is going so fast that if you fell overboard, you will never catch up, I shall lose you. And the sea is very deep. Please do as the Skipper asks you, which is my rule. OK with you?"

"Yes," said Rascal, desperate to be a good crew.

"First we must say 'goodbye' to Eva-three-tons-only, and cast off. Steer towards that house. Bye Eva, see you later, and Eva," he shouted, "don't let that dinghy knock you about."

And so Rascal, as we shall now call him, set off on his adventure and discovered a whole new world.

As they went down the sheltered Kyle, the Skipper put up the mainsail and then the jib, as Rascal held the boat into the wind for him.

All was set and the wind took hold of the sails and blew them out into the open sea.

Rascal had never known such speed, as they creamed their way across the open water towards Arran. The mountains of Arran had seemed misty in the distance. Now, they grew slowly higher until they loomed up over the boat, heavy on their rocky base of sea swept rock.

There was a narrow gap which opened up into a small locken, with a castle at the head of it perched on a spit of sand. This was where they picked up a mooring for the night. After all that wind in his face, Rascal managed to eat half a bowl of Cheerios, and went to sleep with his nose on the table.

The Skipper wrapped him in a blanket and tucked him up in a bunk.

"What a dear little chap you are," he said to himself, "we shall enjoy our trip together."

CHAPTER 3

When he woke in the morning, Rascal was not sure where he was. He sat up, rubbed his eyes, and looked across the cabin to where the Skipper was still snoring in his bunk.

Carefully, Rascal climbed out of his blanket, and tiptoed over. He ran his finger down Skipper's nose. Then he gently lifted one eyelid. Nothing happened. He lifted the corner of Skipper's blanket and crept in beside the sleeping body. Rascal had never known such comforting warmth, he felt it surge through him. He put his head in the crook of Skipper's arm and dozed off. Then he began to snore too.

Eventually, they woke and Rascal had half a packet of Cheerios for breakfast, because he was so hungry and he had never eaten anything so delicious in his whole life.

"Now," said Skipper, "we are off to Campbeltown. This was once the centre of the herring fishing trade, but they fish for herrings no more. By the way Rascal, does your mother know you are with me? She may be worried."

"Oh, sea urchins don't bother with mothers," said Rascal. "They just drop us off and everyone swims away."

"I see," said Skipper, trying not to look surprised, "well while you are being a boy, and I am responsible for your safety on my boat, I had better be like your father."

Rascal thought about this for a while, "Excuse me, but don't you think you are rather old," he said.

"That's a point, I will be your grandfather then." agreed Skipper.

And once they had tied up in the harbour, they cooked supper together. They ate prawns, Rascal knew all about these, and they had new potatoes which were a delicious novelty to Rascal, and spinach which he thought was sea weed, and in his opinion, it would have been better fed to crabs. But when he tasted strawberries, well, he wasn't sharing those with anyone, they tasted heavenly.

CHAPTER 4

From Campbeltown, you can sail south to Ireland, or round the Mull of Kintyre, and set off to the north. Both are dangerous places for sea urchins. The tides round Ireland could sweep you up and carry you miles away down the Irish Sea. And the Mull is even worse, its promontory sticks out into the tides as they rush down, and this makes the water boil and swirl.

Rascal knew of urchins who had been caught up in the huge whirlpools deep down in the sea and were unable to get out. They had become easy prey for the gannets that dived for them there and they were never heard of again.

Coming from the sea, Rascal's skin was already a bit green, but at the thought of the Mull he went quiet, and a shade greener than normal.

"What's up with you?" asked Skipper. Rascal explained how frightened he was of the waters round the Mull.

"Well that is why it is so important to clip yourself onto my boat," said Skipper, "then I will never lose you. Don't worry, we shall be fine, the wind is behind us and we shall set off when the tide turns, and it will help to take us along. We shall be safe and it will be an exhilarating ride."

And so it was.

Rascal watched the water with fascination as they made their way through it. The colour changed, from blue to grey and at times it became silvery and oily. There were no big waves, but every now and then gusts of wind ruffled the water. Where the tides met the water was more turbulent, he fancied that some parts seemed slightly higher, as if they were being pushed up, and then dragged down again.

Birds were fishing all around the boat. Big gannets were falling spectacularly into the sea, and little rafts of guillemots popped up and down on the waves.

Skipper kept well away from the high cliffs on the head of the Mull. He explained to Rascal, "Well, the sea is quieter nearer the cliffs, but if the wind changed, and our motor did not work, we could be in trouble, even blown onto the rocks. I like to sail a couple of miles out to sea with plenty of room to manoeuvre."

By the evening after a long sail, they entered Port Ellen on the Isle of Islay and tied up to a pontoon in the busy harbour.

CHAPTER 5

In the morning Rascal looked about him. There were a number of big fishing boats, with scallop dredgers hanging over the sides. Their cruel metal wheels made Rascal shiver, but then his attention turned to the ferry. It was busy loading a long queue of cars and lorries into its big insides. He skipped off Skipper's boat, made his way carefully round the side of the harbour and watched as the cars drove on board. Some had to go up a ramp to a higher deck and huge lorries and buses filled the lower deck.

"Now then boy, you'll get run over, join the pedestrian queue where you are safe," and with that a big, fat man, picked Rascal up and carried him over to a walkway.

"I'll look after him," said a kind old lady, "Where is your mummy, dear?"

Rascal did not want to find himself on the ferry and he did not like having his hand held either. He was far too independent for that, so he had to make a plan to escape back to Skipper.

"That's my Dad, no, my Grandad over there," he exclaimed pointing toward the harbour wall. And as the kind lady looked up, she loosened her grip on his hand. Rascal spun round and dodged his way down the queue of people, he twisted in and out of the cars as they honked their horns at him, ran along the harbour wall and jumped down onto the pontoon. There was his boat and safety.

"You will fall in the sea running about like that," protested a fisherman.

I don't care if I do, Rascal thought, I am a sea urchin and the sea holds no threats for me.

But when he got back onboard, he had a surprise, "Today, we are going on a bike ride." said Skipper.

CHAPTER 6

"A bike! What is a bike? Why a bike ride. I have never even seen a bike, I don't know what to do!" said Rascal in alarm.

But he need not have worried, the bike man showed him how to steer, and lowered the saddle until he could reach the pedals. He reminded Rascal to use the break on the back wheel so he could stop safely. They had a wobbly practice, and then they were off up the road to explore the island.

"Take it steadily," shouted Skipper, but Rascal felt the wind in his face and went faster and faster, luckily there was a hill ahead or he would have had a painful crash.

Up, up the narrow hill road they went. Sheep jumped up out of the ditches in alarm and bounced away, shaggy brown highland cows looked up but they never stopped chewing. Even so, the cows did nudge their calf to look at this boy, peddling away up the hill on a bike. Rascal thought their long horns sticking out of their foreheads looked like the handlebar of his bike.

And as he looked down, he spotted all the wonderful flowers along the roadside. Bright orange, and yellow patches of birdsfoot-trefoil glowed among the sheep grazed grass.

Almost growing in the dry road were the small white flowers of Bedstraw and mixed in with them the delicate blue flowering stems of Milkwort. Hidden quietly on the sides of the ditch were the single gentle blue flowers of Butterwort held on a thin stem above a rosette of pale leaves, that clung to the soil. The yellow spires of Bog Asphodel were there too, and every now and then. the taller pink spike of an orchid, and the russet brown flowers of Water Avens nodded in the wind above them.

They passed a strange stone standing up in a small field, and Skipper explained that it had been put there in ancient times at the start of civilisation. Then further on, slabs were laid in the shape of a long box, Skipper explained that it could be an ancient burial place, but Rascal thought the man must have been very short to have fitted in it.

At last, they reached the summit of the hill, and there was the sea spread out all round them. It sparkled in the late afternoon sun, and they could see other people sailing along in their boats.

"Epic!" said Rascal.

"Time to go back," said Skipper, and taking care to keep Rascal safely behind him, they made their way carefully down the steep and winding road. In the warm sun the smell of heather and sheep wafted over them. "This is my first expedition on land," Rascal shouted to Skipper, "I like being a boy with you." And he took his feet off the pedals, stuck his legs out straight, and freewheeled gently down the hill.

CHAPTER 7

Rascal had such an appetite for Cheerios that they needed more for breakfast next day. And he had eaten up all the strawberries and drunk all the milk.

It was sunny and quiet in the early morning as they walked down the street to the village shop. Inside the shop, there was a mixture of all the smells you can imagine, biscuits, fruits, vegetables and soap. The shop keeper was laying out the newspapers. He turned round, "Can I help you this fine morning?"

"Yes please," said Skipper, and sent Rascal scurrying round collecting up all the stores they needed, then he gave Rascal some money and asked him to pay the bill.

Rascal looked at the coins in amazement, he had never seen money before and did not understand about paying for things because under the sea, you just helped yourself to what you wanted. Looking uncertain, he put the money in the shopping bag.

"Do it this way..." said Skipper. "Give the money to the shop keeper, and he will give you the things we have bought. Hopefully, he will not need all that money so he will give you back some change. Then you can buy one small packet of Jelly Tots with it, and give the rest back to me."

"You are a lucky little lad today." said the shop keeper.

I wonder what Jelly Tots are, thought Rascal, they sound like a treat to me. He shared these delicious treats with Skipper as they walked back to their boat, but he ate most of them.

That day they set sail for the island of Gigha. It was a sunny balmy day with the wind on the beam. Rascal took the helm, Skipper set the sails perfectly, and the boat sailed just beautifully.

CHAPTER 8

In no time at all, Gigha appeared on the horizon, and they arrived in a beautiful bay of white sand. Rascal picked up a mooring with his long hook as Skipper sailed the boat slowly beside it, then Skipper ran forward and tied them on properly. Rascal looked at the mooring and was reminded of his friend Eva-three-tons-only, and how patient and beautiful she was. The water was clear, he could see the sand below and seaweed clinging to the chain.

Then he heard the sound of boys laughing as they splashed through the water in the shallows.

"Skipper, can I go and play?" he asked, and with that he dived down into the water and swam towards the boys. They got a surprise when his head popped up beside them.

"Hi," said Rascal, "Can I play with you?" Then he did a somersault in the water, sank to the bottom and lay like a star fish on the sand. Up he came shaking the water from his hair and they all laughed.

A brave boy, called Robert, copied him and came up spluttering, another tried but could not sink, so they all decided to run up and down in the waves. Then they sat in the water and kicked their feet, they ran up the sand and had a fight, and back again in the water, until they were worn out.

There was a grassy mound to loll on.
"What is your name?" asked Robert, "and did you come in on that boat?"
"My name is Rascal, and that is my boat."
"I wish I could go on a boat," said Robert.
"I am sure Skipper would invite you on our boat. We could swim over to it."
"You must be joking," said Robert, "I can't swim that far." And this made Rascal realise that he was a special lucky boy, equally at home, on land and sea.
"I'll ask Skipper to pump up the dinghy for you." he offered.
Later that evening, Skipper had four boys helping him row the dinghy in zigzag patterns all over the bay. Then, they came aboard.

CHAPTER 9

Full of happiness, Rascal gazed at his new found friends as they sat in the cockpit together. They cleared up the last of his jelly tots, and polished off packets of crisps which they washed down with coke. The inevitable happened, someone did a burp, then there was a giggle and another did a better burp and it developed into a competition.

"Enough!" said Skipper, "let's show you round the boat."

They explored the boat from top to toe, they lay on the bunks to see how it felt and wriggled down into the pilot bunk under the cockpit, knocking their heads on the roof in their excitement.

Robert was amazed at the kitchen, "It's called a galley in a boat," explained Rascal proudly. He showed them how the cooker could swing on gimbals, so it stayed level when they were at sea and where the cups and plates were stacked securely in special racks. The boys pumped the curious water taps and learned how to open the cupboard doors by putting their finger through the small round hole in them, and finding the latch behind.

They made their way forward and there was the tiny loo. "It's called the heads," Rascal told them, "and you can shut both the doors and wash in the basin on the other side." Then he showed them how to flush the loo by cranking the handle ten times. They all had a go.

A curious boy called Callum, popped his head round the second door, and there in the bows of the boat were no end of sails packed away in their bags. Boat hooks and oars lay along one side, and on the other was another sleeping place, it was slung like a hammock between two poles. He lay down on it, "This is just what I imagine extra special camping would be like, I am so comfy, that I am dropping off to sleep." And he gave them a demo of his loudest snoring. But not for long, he was soon tipped out as everyone wanted to try this special bunk.

The evenings are long during summer in the Western Isles, but it was becoming chilly so Skipper found a packet of chocolate biscuits to keep everyone going and rowed them back to shore in the dinghy. Later he and Rascal sat in the cockpit enjoying a good mug of hot chocolate. "I wonder what camping is?" said Rascal, "My friends are camping, I would like to do that. And do you know, I have never had friends before, I hope we meet them again."

CHAPTER 10

Leepy joined Rascal on the boat during the night.
That night was most exciting. Rascal was fast
asleep in his bunk when he felt his face being
tickled. He gave it a smack, and felt
something whiskery.

"Ouch, careful," said a low gruff voice. Rascal
sat up in alarm to see a rather large pussy cat
with a fine set of stiff whiskers, and bright orange
stripes all over his body.

"I am Leepy," said the whiskers, "Robert's friend.
He has been telling me about you, so I have come
to see you. I am magic, you know. I am so magic
that I can go anywhere and I can do anything and
at any time. I wonder if you would be so kind as to
take me with you to your underwater world. I just
want a peep. Can we go now while Robert sleeps,
secretly, just you and me?" Leepy flourished his
long tail, stretched luxuriantly and yawned hugely,
showing his magnificent teeth.

Rascal was scared at this show of strength, but on the other hand, he would be so proud to show off his watery world.

"Can you really just go under water, like I do?" he asked.

"Oh yes," said Leepy, "I can go anywhere. I have sat on the moon, do you know, it was freezing cold and dusty. And I have spun round in space, hanging on to the tail of a comet. We went into orbit right round the sun and nearly got fried up in the heat. I have visited all the planets," he began to list them, "Pluto, Jupiter, Mars... Actually it was exhausting, they are so far away. So you see, a dip in the ocean is easy."

Leepy followed Rascal. They slid over the side of the boat, and sank down to the sand below. The seaweed waved gently around them as they set off. They floated between the anchor chains from the boats above, then over the eelgrass growing in the shallow sandy water and out of the bay into the deep water of the Sound.

Along the edge was a thick forest of the long straps of Kelp, home to fish, whose silvery sides caught the light from the moon above. Above them floated Jellyfish, their mantles pulsating to a steady rhythm. Rascal spied a lobster pot, but there was nothing in it. They followed the line to the next one and there was a big Langoustine. He reared up in fright and waved his sharp claws at them, but they left him in peace, or you could say to his fate when the pot was hauled in.

Exhausted, the friends returned to the bay and lay on the sand underwater looking up at the stars. As the surface of the water moved, the stars moved too, and as the water stretched and contracted the stars did too, becoming long and thin, then morphing into roundness and even losing their centres. Even the outlines of the hills at the side began to move. "I'd better go back," said Leepy, "or Robert may need me."

CHAPTER 11

Rascal and Skipper raised the anchor early next morning and set off north. It was a good beam reach with a south west wind.

"This will give us a nice comfortable ride, and with the tide going with us, a speedy one too," said Skipper. As they went up the outside of the rocky bulk of the Kintyre peninsula, inlets kept opening up to them. Rascal longed to explore them.

"Another time," said Skipper, "We have a long way to go to the Isle of Skye.

"This is West Loch Tarbert on our starboard. It is an interesting loch and goes towards Tarbert Harbour on Loch Fyne. Tarbert is an ancient Viking name for a place where the Vikings would row their boats up a loch and into the river at its head. Then they carried their boats overland so that they could go down the river the other side. It made an excellent short cut and they could attack people by surprise.

"But this Tarbert has a special history to it. In 1093, Edgar the Third of Scotland agreed with Magnus Barefoot, (can you believe his name) who was the son of the Viking king of Norway, that he would allow them to rule all the Western Isles of Scotland, provided there was peace at last. Well, Magnus Barefoot was cunning, to claim the Kintyre peninsular, he rowed up West Loch Tarbert, then sat in his boat with his paddle while his men carried him the short distance over to East Loch Tarbert. Then he claimed that Kintyre was an island as he had been between it and the mainland in a boat!

"In reality, the arrangement lasted less than 200 years, as Norway ceded the Western Isles to the Scottish crown in 1266.

"But Kintyre has been endlessly fought over, Robert, the Bruce, arrived in 1306 and built a castle in Tarbert where he took refuge, and that too is now in ruins. Fights over religion were waged and there was an appalling massacre of more than 300 members of the McDonald and Irish McDougall clans at Dunaverty Castle in 1647. They were tricked into surrender and their bodies thrown into the sea. But there is a saying, 'Kintre is 40 miles long, and every mile is beautiful.' Perhaps that is why people fight over it and its white sand beaches.

"Soon we shall pass Loch Sween. We must be careful of the rocks in its approaches, and there is one small island, Eilean Mor, where one of Saint Columba's monks lived all on his own. This was long ago when the story of Christ first came to Britain."

"I can see his chapel on the side of the bay," said Rascal, gazing through the binoculars. "It was not actually his chapel, but would have been built later," said Skipper, "The monk would have spent his time in prayer, he lived in a small round cell and wore rough wool clothes. His life was one of abstinence. But do you know, not so long ago, this island was so secret and remote that it was used to distil whiskey, doing this was against the law and a dangerous thing to do."

"I have heard from sea living folk that there are fairies around here," said Rascal, beginning to feel anxious, "they say that they live on some beautiful islands and tempt sea folk towards them with soft music. But as they get near, the tide changes. The water swirls round and sweeps them onto muddy banks where they are trapped, flapping and helpless. Many die and are easy-pickings for seagulls, and even worse, there are herons with their dagger beaks. If you don't mind, let's press on Skipper."

Rascal was so anxious to move on, that he helmed the boat immaculately, steering a careful course, and keeping the sails filled with wind. And when the wind dropped between the cloudbanks coming in from the ocean, his eyes narrowed and fingers clenched round the tiller, and so, they made good time past the entrance to the Crinan Canal, and on to Ardfern, where they spent the night. *One day, thought Rascal, I would like to go through that canal, then I would be almost on land like a real boy. I could get off the boat and run down the path and help to open the loch gates.*

CHAPTER 12

To get in and out of Ardfern is a challenge due to the Dorus Mor which means the 'great gate' in Gaelic. This is a deep channel with strong tides and you need to sail with the tide, or at slack water to get through. So Skipper timed his departure from Ardfern carefully and Rascal watched the small standing waves in the current in fascination as he fantasised about his journey through the Crinan Canal. *I could run into the fields at the sides of the canal and explore the woods. I think I would find lots of friends.* Rascal remembered the fun he had had with the boys on the Isle of Gigha. But this was no time for day dreaming, on the far side of the Sound was the dreaded Gulf of Corryvreckan that divides the Isles of Jura and Scarba with an even stronger tidal race.

Rascal had heard tales about this place too, that it had a deep bottomless hole, where an old hag, the Goddess of Winter called Cailleach Bheur sat and washed her great colourful plaid until there was no colour left and it was quite white. It took her three days and she settled to her task in wild noisy weather. Then she turned her plaid into snow and in winter she put its chilly grip onto the land and sea. The story filled him with dread.

"We will not go in there," said Skipper, "When the tide begins to run the water swirls in dangerous whirlpools, the tide surges through the gulf at up to eight knots, and there are dangerous down currents as the water swirls round underwater cliffs. You have seen standing waves as we have made our way through the Dorus Mor. Well, in the Corryvreckan, they can be much taller, twice my height, and they can go on and on out into the Ocean towards the Garvellach Islands. It is a dangerous place, and not for us."

"I don't suppose you have heard about the Norse king called Breacan?" Skipper continued. "He was showing off to his girlfriend by taking his boat near a whirlpool. It was such a stupid thing to do, he was dragged in and drowned. Later, his body was thrown up on the shore, and they say his dog found it and rescued him, but he was dead of course. There is a legend that the Old Hag was involved and she dragged him and his boat down under the water with a rope made of hemp, wool and virgin's hair."

As they sailed their way north past the entrance to the Gulf, Rascal peered between its steep sides, the water looked calm but he fancied he heard the roar of the rushing water, and the wicked high-pitched cackle of the old Hag. This place was not called the cauldron of the speckled sea for nothing. Its rushing water made it dangerous for those that lived in the ocean as he did, as well as for those who sailed on its surface.

CHAPTER 13

Now the fog crept in. Everything went still, the wind dropped to nothing. It became difficult to see where the water gave way to fog and the outlines of the low islands on each side of the Sound of Luing faded away. The water surface was motionless but the tide still carried the boat northwards, very slowly. Rascal could hear a lamb calling its mother in the distance, then the engine of a car and somebody banging metal but he could see nothing. Skipper was concentrating hard, plotting his course carefully and checking off the marker buoys as they made the safe passage up the middle of the Sound. He left the Isle of Scarba and Lunga on the west and the gentle slopes of Luing could just be seen on the east. Rascal spotted the lighthouse on the low island of Lunga as it popped through the fog then faded away again.

South of the lighthouse, between Scarba and Lunga is the Grey Dogs Channel, where the tide can run so fast between the islets in the channel that the sea turns into a torrent and drops like a river, but Rascal was becoming accustomed to the idea of dangerous places. There was no choice but to motor and it felt slow and tedious. Then they began to hear the sounds of human activity as they neared Oban. *We are nearly there*, thought Rascal. But no, they had to carry on to the west of the Isle of Kerrera and past the Grey Isles before they could turn into the Sound of Mull. Rascal had a peep at the chart and it did not look too far. He could just see Duart castle, sitting high up on a promontory on the island of Mull at the entrance to the Sound of Mull. But they had to continue further north before turning to make their way between the Redire islands and the mainland. *Why can't we cut across?* thought Rascal.

When they turned into the Sound of Mull everything changed. The tide was against them and the wind got up. It was blowing right down the Sound and poor little Rascal was tired. But he kept his course, pressing onto the tiller and leaning into the wind as they made their way under the green cliff face of the mainland.

"Look out for the ruin near the shore," shouted Skipper, "Soon after that, we can turn into Loch Aline."

Rascal picked it out with relief, then as the entrance of Loch Aline came into view, he could not wait to turn in. But Skipper came up from below in haste. "No, no," he said, "Keep out until we can see clearly through the Loch entrance or we will be in danger from a line of rocks on the starboard side." Rascal gritted his teeth and carried on west ward. How relieved he was when Skipper said, "Now go!"

You cannot believe how calm and lovely it was in that Loch. It felt like heaven. Rascal was so tired that he curled up in a rug and slept while Skipper cooked supper.

CHAPTER 14

Next morning Loch Aline revealed its secrets. A light mist rose off the surface of the glassy water, and a workboat chugged through making ripples that fanned out and gently lifted the sleeping boats one by one. As his boat settled, Rascal looked up the loch to where a small river fanned its way across mud and gravel. It was dotted with herons, their backs hunched and beaks held horizontally, but their eyes were on the water as it slowly rose with the tide. *They are waiting for a tasty morsel to wriggle by,* thought Rascal. Then quick as flash, a beak jabbed down and a heron threw his head back as he gulped down his prize. The others stood motionless and patient.

Along the shore tall trees hung over the dark water of the loch, water droplets dripping from their leaves made gentle ringlets on the surface. But something else was happening, a hump lifted up then gently dropped down and round, up and round it went, did a twiddle then round again. "Ah," said Rascal quietly, "Master otter is hunting for his breakfast, I know about otters."

Then Rascal noticed an odd looking upright rock on the end of a gravel spit. "A sheep out there," he wondered. As he did so, it moved its head and he realised it was a sea eagle. Feeling anxious and excited, he called Skipper to look.

"Wow," said Skipper, "that is the first one I have ever seen, I have heard that people are trying to reintroduce them here. Isn't he enormous?"

"I have heard," said Rascal, "that they can just spot you from the sky, then they swoop down and pick you out of the sea. That makes me nervous."

"Don't worry," consoled Skipper, "you are too big even for them." And so the two friends settled down in the sun in the cockpit for breakfast. But suddenly, there was a great roar and banging as a big truck bounced out of a yard on the side of the cliff beside them. It was piled with heaps of white sand.

"What a truck!" said Rascal gazing in amazement.

"There is a drift mine here," said Skipper, "that truck is going into the hill to dig out some more sand. The sand is so pure that it can be made into glass that is used in special instruments. I was told that there are two galleries, and the older lower one is now flooded with water. The upper gallery has a small lake that once had a boat on it.

They use the lake water to sort the sand by the size of each grain. This is a process where water is made to flow upwards through the sand. I am trying to think if the biggest grains will be at the top or the bottom. What do you think? But it is such a simple process, isn't it clever?

But that mine is totally dark, the darkness wraps quietly round you until you have no sense of yourself. I went in the entrance once with a torch and quickly its light became nothing. I felt so insecure that I dared not put a foot down to go forward and the silence thundered around me. Luckily, I had walked in beside the wall and by fingering my way along it I made my way back with my heart pounding."

CHAPTER 15

It was time to start the journey up the Sound of Mull for Tobermory. The sun shone and they zigzagged their way up the Sound with a long tack to starboard and then Rascal felt as if they were going backwards on the opposite tack. It was a long sail but the cheerfully coloured houses along the water line finally came into view and they turned into Tobermory Bay.

Two cheerful young men came by in a dinghy. "Do you want to see the puffins?"

"Puffins!" said Rascal, "Yes please!"

Next morning, they joined a motor boat that was able to get them ashore among the shallow water and rocks around the Treshnish Islands.

These islands are a safe place to breed for many sea birds, but especially puffins whose nests are in burrows in the ground. The puffins flew in right above Rascal's head, not a bit frightened, and landed in front of him, skidding on their heels to a stop. Then to show they were in control, they did a little jump, stood upright, gave Rascal a look and waddled into their front door. One had some grass for his nest in his beak, he looked comical and serious with his round eyes and colourful beak.

"Come on," said Skipper, "there is more to see," and turning the corner an amazing sight met their eyes. It was a colony of Guillemots clinging to the side of a cliff. They were so tightly packed that every now and then one dropped off and had to fly back and push in. The cliff opposite the Guillemots' had ledges on it and here kittiwakes, small gulls with grey backs and white fronts, were sitting on their nests. Rascal thought it would be so easy for the eggs to roll off these narrow ledges, but Skipper explained that the eggs were carefully shaped with a pointed end which helps to keep them in the nest.

"There is one sea bird here which nests on its own," said Skipper, "If we look in the rocks, we might be lucky." And they were, they found a Razorbill, which hissed at them to go away. It was black, like the Guillemots and surprisingly large. Rascal could have stayed watching this wonderland filled with birds flying in and out all day, but it was time to move on to Fingal's Cave on Staffa Island.

Skipper knew all about the music written by Mendelsohn, and as the swell of the ocean gently lifted in and sucked out of the cave, he thought how lucky he was to be there in the cheerful sunshine. Rascal was amazed at the columns of rock; they were big enough for two people to sit on and had eight regular sides. The whole of the island seemed to be made of them. They formed high cliffs round the cave, and he could see more of them in the clear water, where they were broken off and encrusted with barnacles.

"It is said," said Skipper, "that these columns run under the sea all the way to Ireland, where they reappear as the Giant's Causeway. And there is another tale about feuding Scottish and Irish giants."

CHAPTER 16

"The next leg of our journey," said Skipper, "is round Ardnamurchan Point and on to the safety of Mallaig harbour. Luckily the wind is with us, the weather forecast is good and off we go. But I shall keep well away from the cliffs, I feel safer that way, you never know what will happen at sea, and we shall be more exposed to the Atlantic Ocean now."

They turned out of Tobermory bay, and sailed past groups of guillemots bobbing on the waves, who dived in the water as the boat approached. Suddenly, there was a furious panic ahead of the boat. Jumping up, Rascal could see an Eider duck, frantically encouraging her ducklings to dive under the water as a sea eagle swooped down to grab one for his breakfast. Rascal joined in, shouting and waving his arms. His help was just what was needed, it was too much for the eagle and it flew off, and as the boat sailed on Rascal looked back and watched the mother duck leading her brood away. *All that water, tiny birds and no hiding place*, he thought.

The swell increased as they met the open sea and to Rascal's delight, three dolphins joined them, playing in the water that creamed around them. Gannets circled the air high above, then dived headfirst onto their prey. Rascal wondered, *how they could see anything in the water at that height?* He then watched carefully for each one to surface after its dive.

Then, off Ardnamurchan Point, and swimming parallel to it, Rascal saw three fins making their way steadily south towards the Isles of Coll and Tiree. In excitement he called Skipper, "Whales, three of them, come and look."

They were huge and dark, but not whales. "Those are basking sharks," said skipper, "they swim along with their mouths open hoovering up plankton, and they are not dangerous and cannot bite even though they are called sharks. This is a favourite place of theirs'. I have seen them here before. Well spotted, young man."

Slowly, as they rounded the Point, the outline of the three Small Isles came into view. In front was Muck which is small, green and low, and behind it rose Eigg with its high spine made of hard basalt. Its outline looked like the teeth of a saw against the grey sky. And behind again the high, but softer outline of the mountains of Rhum, this is the largest of the islands. Out to the northwest is Canna, green and fertile, but they could not see it as they made their way north to Mallaig.

They did not stop, but passed the bright white bay of Sanna, then further to the east the entrance to the beautiful Loch Moidart with Eilean Shona at the entrance, the Borrodale islands and Loch nan Ceall with Arisaig at its head and so to Mallaig.

CHAPTER 17

Mallaig has traffic lights at the entrance to the port, so they were glad to see them turn green and allow them in. The port had been built for trawlers and larger boats, and in past times had been busy with a rail link to take fish south. It felt cavernous, the quays were huge solid platforms that ran out into the black water, there were ladders fixed on the sides and no railings. It was a long way down. Poor old Skipper was tired and once they had settled in, he went fast asleep in the cockpit. Rascal could not wait to explore, he popped his head in the sheds smelling of fish and the sea, and found the huge silo filled with ice that the trawlers used. Everywhere felt deserted. Running out on the quays was scary and made his legs feel wobbly. But he could see a boy, and this boy was buzzing round on a homemade scooter.

"Got this old geezer's scooter," the boy explained, "He didn't want it no more, an' I put big wheels on, an' hotted-up the engine. Goes a treat! Watch me!" With that, he sped off, did a circuit and stopped abruptly at the edge of the quay. Rascal was terrified.

"How do you stop?" he asked,

"Just cut the engine, see. Got no brakes. Only put it together last night and I am tryin' it out. Want a go? Boyo."

"Not today, thank you." Replied Rascal very quietly. Wanting to change the subject, he asked politely, "Excuse me, but do you live here?"

"In a manner of speakin. Stationed here, see. I'm a trawler man, but Mallaig is so quiet I'm thinkin' of moving on."

"What's it like on a trawler?" asked Rascal, as he thought of the boats that trawled for scallops from Tarbert.

"It's alright," said the boy, "We go way out you see, beyond the Outer Hebrides, there is a lot more swell out there and when it is windy the waves can crash right over the deck. There you are getting in the net and it is one hand for you and the other for the boat. And it is very cold," he went quiet for a moment and rolled his eyes up to the sky, "Icy, it can get icy cold. In January, when they are about, the Orcas are so cunnin', they follow close to the net and feast on everythin' that falls out of the trawl as we bring it in."

"Orca whales would scare me," said Rascal in awe of his new friend casually describing his life.

"Awe, they're all right," said the trawler boy, "You should see the seals. They are right cheeky. They will swim right in the net and take a fish. One after another."

"Wow."

"And the gannets too, they dive all 'round the trawl."

"You would think that they would get a headache with all that diving from such heights," mused Rascal, remembering them all circling and plunging into the sea around Ardnamurchan Point.

"That diving makes them go blind in the end," said the boy, "You see them just swimming about on the surface of the sea. Can't dive no more, can't feed you see and they starve. Not very old either, only about four or five. Sad end really for such a beautiful bird. You never bin on a boat then, little lad?" he asked.

"Oh yes," replied Rascal, "I am a crew member on a yacht with Skipper."

"Lucky you."

"Actually, I am a sea urchin, but please keep in to yourself, as at the moment I am being a boy."

"You OK with me. A sea urchin. I've heard of them. Magic, aren't they. You got any magic?"

"I hope when I get older that I will get some." replied Rascal. "But magic things happen to me, like being a boy and getting about a bit. But I would like to be as brave as you, and dare to go fishing in the deep sea."

CHAPTER 18

Time was running out, Skipper needed to get home but he was determined to catch the tide running north through the Sound of Sleat so that he could anchor in Plockton Bay north of the Isle of Skye, before he returned home.

Luckily the wind was southwest so they had a comfortable sail up the Sound between the Isle of Skye and the Mainland. Soon Loch Nevis opened up to the east on the mainland, it looked so beautiful and tempting with its high mountains, but they had no time to explore it.

"You have to be careful in there," said Skipper, "You get fierce squalls when the wind turns southerly. Now we shall pass the Knoydart peninsular, one of the wildest and most remote places in Scotland. I would like to sail up into Loch Hourn which opens up next. I have been told that it is particularly spectacular at its head, but you have to sail through four sets of narrows to get there and be very careful. The mountains tower over you 2000 feet high, and like Loch Nevis you can get violent squalls and even katabatic winds."

"What is a katabatic wind?" asked Rascal.

Skipper had to think hard as he tried to explain. "Well, the prevailing west wind blows air onto the high slopes at the back of the loch. These mountain tops are cold, even snow covered, they cool the air down, this makes the air heavier and it falls rapidly down the slope of the mountain to the valley below causing a wind. The wind is rough and unpredictable, and the speed increases as it funnels down the loch. This is the wild Highlands you know. Now how about a cup of tea."

Rascal popped down below, he had become quick at these little tasks, and put the kettle on. Suddenly, Skipper called him up into the cockpit.

"Look, Rascal, I can just see the Sandaig Islands ahead of us. Gavin Maxwell lived here with wild otters and wrote an amazing book about it called 'Ring of Bright Water'. Oh, I must tell you, Rascal, I have so much enjoyed having you on my boat and showing you all these places. You are as good as a real boy."

Rascal felt a surge of pleasure as he heard this. He had met several otters in the sea and even tried to keep up with them as they turned and twisted in the water with such speed and grace, but he did not think they would have been able to sail like him.
Yes, how lucky he was.

The Sound had narrowed to half its width, and soon they would enter Kyle Rhea, the narrow channel of over a mile that ran between the Mainland and the Isle of Skye. The tide was with them, as it always has to be for sailing boats, and was moving through at eight knots. Rascal could feel it pick the boat up and carry it along. The westerly wind blowing over the steep slopes on the Skye side picked up the faint scent of the pine trees and blew it in gusts down on the boat. It was heaven.

Too soon it was over, the water slowed, the channel opened up and there was Loch Alsh ahead of them. The north side of the loch was busy with people, roads, a port and railway. But Skipper asked Rascal to take the helm and head to the west so that they could pass under the new bridge that links the Isle of Skye to the Mainland.

It was not far from the bridge to Plockton where Skipper planned to anchor for the night. But Rascal was tired, Skipper was down below checking his charts, because they had to be so careful making their way up and round the many rocks that help shelter this beautiful anchorage. Rascal longed to take a short cut, but knew he must go right out in the bay before turning in.

The light was going as they laid the anchor, and they sat in the cockpit eating their supper and watching the ring of lights in the village. Rascal thought how delicious boys' food was and what a good cook Skipper was too. He was getting a taste for grilled steak and lamb chops followed by strawberries and cream. Not that there was much wrong with raw scallops under water wrapped round with a leaf of seaweed.

Rascal had just one more night on the boat with Skipper, tomorrow they would make their way south, back the way they had come.

CHAPTER 19

Skipper planned to leave his boat at Armadale
on the Isle of Skye. It is a safe place for his boat
as there is a boat yard in a little bay, and then he
has a short ferry ride over to Mallaig where he
catches his train bound for home.

So the next day, they left their peaceful mooring
and retraced their steps southwards. They caught
the tide as it ran south through the Kyle of Rhea,
but found that the wind was southerly and blowing
right at them. Their passage was tough as the
boat banged up and down against the short sharp
waves caused by wind against tide. A cold mist
blew in their faces, and with tiring regularity, a
wind sprung up, followed by a wet cold dose
of rain.

Tired out, they relaxed as the Sound widened out. Skipper decided that they had earned a good treat and so he set course for the Duisdale Hotel and delicious supper. He was sure Rascal was up to the challenge of sitting up to a meal in a restaurant, and he was not disappointed.

"Is this your grandson?" asked the waitress.

"Are you a good crew?" asked the manager.

"Do you like coca cola?" asked the wine waiter.

"Yes please," replied Rascal, and the waiter folded a huge white napkin over his lap. Then they brought wonderful food on hot plates and he ate very carefully, and far too much, but it was worth it.

After supper they picked their way down the lawn that sloped towards the sea. The wind had dropped, the air was crystal clear, stars covered the dark sky and the new moon was half way on its journey across the sky. Their feet crunched on the shingle beach and slid on the seaweed covered rocks. Into the dinghy and off to the boat. Rascal was glad Skipper did not ask him to row them back, he was so tired but so happy.

Next day, they made it to Armadale and settled the boat on a mooring in a quiet corner. Skipper was anxious that Rascal would be safe while he was away. He left him a good stash of favorite food, and they hid the key to the cabin in a secret place so that Rascal could get in and out.

"There you are, Rascal," he said, "look after yourself. You are at home in the water. You understand the boat. It is just on land that I worry. Be careful, and when I come back, we will sail home and catch up with Eva, our home lady. Here is a chart where you can cross off the days until I return." And with that he gave a cheery wave, and set off for the ferry and the long train ride home.

Rascal stood on deck and watched him until he disappeared round a bend on the track. Then he saw the ferry set off. Skipper had gone. He was alone. Who was he? Where was he? Rascal was not quite sure. He felt a frisson of anxiety run through him as he stood alone on deck watching people busy in the boat yard, walking to the ferry, laughing, kicking stones and chatting to each other, he was not sure how to manage that world and he felt scared.

CHAPTER 20

Two weeks passed, and Skipper found himself back on the train bound for Mallaig and his much loved boat. His friend Doug was with him.

"I have a cabin boy now," he said.

"Really," said Doug, "and what do you mean by that. Has your wife given you yet another toy from the lifeboat stall? Does he clean the deck? I hope he washes up."

The joke passed Skipper by, "Oh yes, he is a super boy, and such a quick learner," he said, "On my trip up to Skye he learned to helm the boat, and even began to read the charts, you wait till you see him when we go aboard. I call him Rascal."

"I see," said Doug, "and what is his real name?"

"Rascal, that's what I call him."

"I can't believe you have left him here alone on the boat for all this time, have you?"

"Oh that's alright, he belongs here." They both relapsed into silence.

Doug thought that was a funny thing to say. *Boys generally belong to someone,* he thought.

"Do his parents know where he is?" he asked. But Skipper had dozed off and there was no reply.

You should have seen the bags of supplies they bought in the Co-op in Mallaig. They struggled onto the ferry with them, then off, then into the service boat that took them over to Skipper's boat where all the bags filled the cockpit.

"What a lot of jelly tots!" said Doug as he emptied a bag.

"Oh yes," replied Skipper, "they are Rascal's favorite sweet, he'll turn up when he hears us bumping about. I expect he has gone for a swim."

They settled in and cooked supper. It was time for bed, but Rascal had not appeared.

"He is probably exploring Skye." said Skipper, "I told him when I would be back, the dark won't worry him." But it did worry Skipper, he had expected Rascal to be eagerly waiting for him, ready to set sail for home.

Next morning, there was still no Rascal, and Skipper became anxious.

"We'll give him a bit more time," he said, "I expect he will be here soon, but we ought to catch the tide this evening."

Doug wanted to set off. "Let's take a walk ashore and see if he is there, maybe he has forgotten the day." So they rowed across the bay and wandered around in a hopeless sort of way. Doug wanted to ask if anyone had seen Rascal, but for some reason, Skipper did not seem a bit keen.

"What does he look like?" he asked, "How old is he? Would he have gone into the village shop for sweets or ice cream? Maybe the shop keeper would have seen him." He began to wonder if this Rascal was a bit of a dream.

"No, no, he really did come with me," said Skipper. He held his hand half way up his body, "He is this tall, with curly hair, and skinny, a big smile and he is rather green." He stopped, "Well, just a bit green tinged, it goes away in the sunshine."

Doug gave him a puzzled look. "Let's get back to the boat," he said.

Late that afternoon they set off for the journey home. Skipper felt so sad, he kept finding reminders of Rascal, some crayons he had bought him, a comic, sweet wrappers and a small toy boat. Was Rascal alright? Was he being a boy or an urchin in the water? Skipper had no way of knowing and was full of worry. He wished that he had not left him alone on the boat.

Doug began to wonder if Skipper had been imagining things on his solitary boat trip. Perhaps the poor old boy was going bonkers! He had heard of sailors having hallucinations in the middle of the Pacific, solo sailors had no one to talk to, perhaps his imagination had run away with him.

EPILOGUE

Eva-three-tons-only was swinging gently on the high tide. She enjoyed being able to see all about her. She felt a tickle on her bottom, then another twitchy sort of tickle. Eva sighed and did a wobble. Then two hands went bum-diddly-bum on her bottom. Eva went pink with pleasure.

"Ah it's you, you've come back, my little urchin," she cooed. And up jumped Rascal onto her head. "I missed you, and Skipper went home so I was alone on the boat, but my friend on the trawler was going south so he gave me a lift," said Rascal, "and here I am."

"And here you will stay, I hope, where you belong," said Eva. "Did you enjoy your trip?"

"Every minute," replied Rascal. "It was such an adventure. But I need to belong to my belonging, to my home, to have you. Yet, it was such fun to play with all those boys. I want it all and I am so tired. I will tell you about it in the morning." With that he slid gently down Eva's chain and curled up in his familiar underwater hole.

Eventually Skipper sailed back up the Kyle to Eva. "I am worried about Rascal," he told her, "I feel so responsible, he has run off. I should not have left him alone. I do not think that I should have even taken him."

"Do not worry, take my word for it," Eva comforted him, "He will be fine."

"He has come home, he has had a wonderful time and now he is where he should be," she said to herself. Eva turned her face to the warm evening sun and felt it caressed by the water lapping round her chin and a contented smile spread from her to her friend, the Skipper. For some reason, he felt reassured.